Barker's Crime

RETOLD & ILLUSTRATED BY

DICK GACKENBACH

Harcourt Brace & Company
SAN DIEGO NEW YORK LONDON

Library of Congress Cataloging-in-Publication Data
Gackenbach, Dick.
Barker's crime/by Dick Gackenbach.—1st ed.
p. cm.
Summary: A hungry stray dog steals the aroma of a greedy man's food and a just punishment is handed down.
ISBN 0-15-200628-1
[1. Dogs—Fiction. 2. Greed—Fiction.]
I. Title.
PZ7.G117Bar 1996
[E]—dc20 94-41419

First edition
A B C D E

Printed in Singapore

To Charlotte Elizabeth Carew Miller

There once lived a greedy man named Mr. Gobble, who, when he wasn't trying to cheat someone, loved to eat. Mr. Gobble had no friends and always ate alone in his garden under a big elm tree.

Each mealtime Mr. Gobble's cook would serve him fine roasts of turkey, ham, beef, and pork. There would be freshly baked breads, sweet biscuits, and berry muffins. And each meal would end with assorted pies and puddings. From all this delicious food a marvelous aroma would fill the garden and float out over the garden wall.

One day as Mr. Gobble was enjoying a delicious sweet potato pie, a hungry stray hound named Barker passed by the garden wall. When that wonderful aroma of food tickled Barker's nose, his tongue popped out and he began to drool from the corners of his mouth. He was a very hungry dog.

Barker ran to the wall and stood on his hind legs. When he saw Mr. Gobble eating, he did as any hungry dog would do—Barker wagged his tail and begged, hoping for a treat. But the sight of the hungry dog only annoyed Mr. Gobble and made him angry.

"Go away, you vile beggar," screamed the selfish man.

But Barker did not go away; he was on the other side of the wall, and he knew he was safe there. Barker remained, sniffing in the tantalizing aroma of Mr. Gobble's food as it floated up over the wall.

Perhaps, Barker thought, *the man will get angry enough to toss a turkey leg at me.* But he was to have no such luck. Not a single crumb of a muffin would Mr. Gobble part with. And so Barker lowered his head and went away.

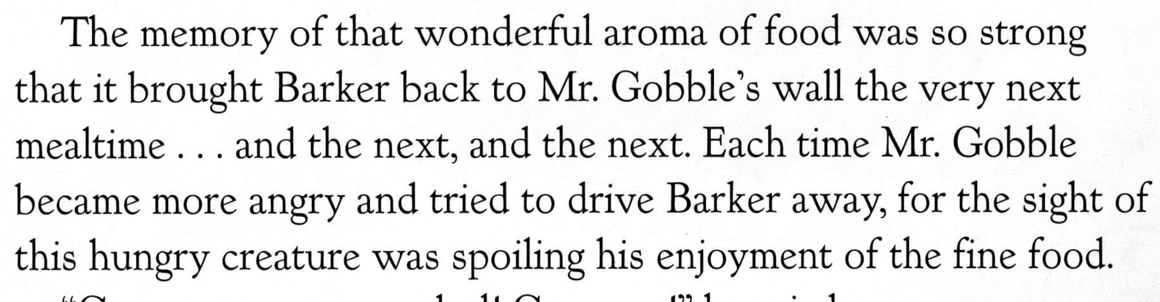

The memory of that wonderful aroma of food was so strong that it brought Barker back to Mr. Gobble's wall the very next mealtime . . . and the next, and the next. Each time Mr. Gobble became more angry and tried to drive Barker away, for the sight of this hungry creature was spoiling his enjoyment of the fine food.

"Go away, you scoundrel! Go away!" he cried.

But Barker remained by the wall, if for no other reason than to sniff the delicious aroma and to drool.

After many days, Mr. Gobble could stand the unwanted visitor no longer. He left his food and went straight to the police.

"I want you to arrest that miserable hound," he demanded.

"What should we arrest him for?" the police wanted to know.

"For stealing," shouted Mr. Gobble.

"For stealing *what?*" they asked.

"The aroma of my food, of course!" insisted Mr. Gobble.

And so, poor Barker was arrested and dragged off to jail. And Mr. Gobble returned to his garden to eat.

Fortunately, when Barker came to trial he appeared before a judge who was known throughout the land to be very fair. Many people came to watch the trial, for most of them had been cheated by Mr. Gobble at one time or another.

"It is my belief," the judge began, "that the aroma of the food was part of the food and so belonged to Mr. Gobble. And since Mr. Gobble did not invite Barker to share his food," he added, "I, therefore, must surmise that the dog stole the aroma."

The crowd booed, and Barker hung his head and put his tail between his legs.

The judge held up his hand and continued, "Since the dog came every day, three times a day, this is a very severe crime. I must give the matter serious thought before I decide what the fair and proper punishment should be."

Poor Barker let out a howl and slid under the table.

"The trial," the judge announced, "will resume tomorrow morning at the scene of the crime."

At sunup the next day, the people gathered by the big elm tree in Mr. Gobble's garden to hear the sentence. The judge arrived last and left his horse by Mr. Gobble's gate. He called the trial to order and commanded Barker and Mr. Gobble to stand before him.

"I have made my decision," he said as he handed Mr. Gobble a long leather whip.

Mr. Gobble was delighted; he was sure the judge would tell him to whip the dog. He took the whip and made several swings through the air. The crowd was silent, and Barker whimpered and trembled with fear.

Then the judge held up his hand. "Wait," he said. He turned slowly toward the crowd. "Does everyone agree," he asked, "that it was the invisible part of the food and, therefore, the spirit, the ghost, the intangible part of the food that was stolen?"

"Yes," the crowd agreed.

"And," the judge asked again, "does everyone agree that the spirit, the ghost, the intangible part of the dog is his shadow?"

"We do!" shouted the crowd.

"Good," said the judge. "Since the crime was against the intangible part of the food, only the intangible part of the dog can be punished."

The crowd cheered the judge's decision. And Barker smiled with relief.

When the crowd calmed down, the judge turned to Mr. Gobble. "The shadow of the dog is big now," he said. "You must beat the shadow until the sun is straight up in the sky. When there is nothing left of the shadow, and only then, will the spirit of the dog be punished."

Mr. Gobble protested. He threw down the whip and withdrew the charges.

The judge shook his head. "You can't do that," he told Mr. Gobble. "You made the charges, you caused the arrest, and you wanted the trial. Now you must carry out the justice." Then the judge warned Mr. Gobble, "And the whip better not touch even one hair on that dog . . ."

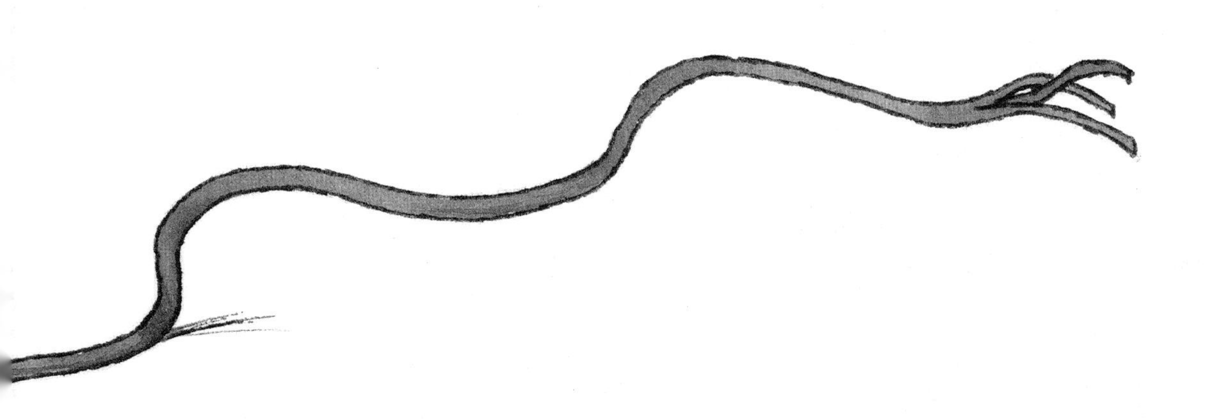

Mr. Gobble had no choice. For hours on end, he whipped the shadow of the dog as the sun slowly rose in the sky. The people laughed and made fun of him, while Barker jumped up and down and yelped, pretending that the blows to his shadow were causing him pain.

As the sun rose, the shadow became smaller. When the shadow was no more than a sliver, Mr. Gobble had to get down on his knees to hit the shadow without touching the dog. After a while, Mr. Gobble was so tired he could barely raise his hand; the whip felt as if it were made of iron. Mr. Gobble was dripping with sweat and covered with dust. He had even hit himself several times while trying to protect the hairs of the dog from the whip. The crowd was roaring with laughter.

Finally, Mr. Gobble could bear the strain no longer. He let out an angry cry and threw the whip away. Then he jumped on the back of the judge's horse and rode out of town as fast as that horse could carry him.

"Good riddance," the crowd called after him.

"And he'd better not come back," said the judge with a chuckle. "Because if he does, I'll arrest him for stealing my best horse."

The greedy Mr. Gobble was never seen again. And as for Barker, he was given the key to Mr. Gobble's pantry, where he, along with his many friends, ate everything in sight.

The illustrations in this book were done in pen and sepia ink
and Dr. Martin's Radiant Concentrated Watercolors on
D'Arches 140-pound cold press watercolor paper.
The text type was set in Kennerly.
Color separations by Bright Arts, Ltd., Singapore
Printed and bound by Tien Wah Press, Singapore
This book was printed with soya-based inks on Leykam recycled paper,
which contains more than 20 percent postconsumer waste
and has a total recycled content of at least 50 percent.
Production supervised by Warren Wallerstein and Ginger Boyer
Designed by Kaelin Chappell